Barkley's Sandbar Christmas Miracle

Christopher Metcalf

TT Tree Tunnel Publishing

For kids. Yours and mine.

'Twas the night before Christmas, when all thru' the house,

Not a creature was stirring, not even a mouse;

The stockings were hung by the chimney with care,

In hopes that St. Nicholas soon would be there.

—Clement C. Moore, 1823

Thank you for believing.

CHAPTER ONE

The water in the Arkansas River flowing southeast through Tulsa, Oklahoma drops to a trickle each winter, like it often does during July and August when it is burning hot outside. During the spring and fall, the water level will sometimes rise to the top of the banks of the river's edge nearly a half-mile wide.

Tulsa would flood regularly until they built the Keystone Dam about 15 miles upstream. The dam keeps the water under control. The result is a bunch of sandbars forming in the middle of the river like islands in a slow moving sea. Some folks think the sandbars are ugly. Visitors will often say "you call this a river?"

What does all this have to do with anything? Well, not much really, unless you believe in miracles.

I've never told this story before.

I never told my late wife, although I'm sure she knew what was up. Never told my kids or their kids or even their kids, my great grandkids. I kept my word to a certain fella who crash-landed on Barkley's Sandbar just after midnight nearly 50 years ago. Barkley kept his word as well.

I remember that night like it was yesterday. I'm no writer, so bear with me...

CHAPTER TWO

Barkley and I liked to take walks late in the evenings. It was our special time together at the end of the day. Barkley, in case you're wondering, is my faithful and truest best friend. He's a giant, and I do mean giant, Great Dane. He's huge, really huge. He's mostly white with big black spots like an enormous Dalmatian on steroids. Did I mention, he is huge.

But when I look at him, I still see the tiny little puppy looking up at me in the pet store. Just like whenever I looked at my wife I could always see the beautiful young woman with bright blue eyes that melted my heart the first time I saw them.

And just like my wife, who I met awhile after Barkley came into my life, it was love at first sight the first time I saw that adorable little puppy. How could something so cute and tiny yelping up at me in his little crate grow to be so big?

My name is Gerald Vaughan, by the way. I was a young attorney working in Tulsa when I found Barkley in a neighborhood pet store in 1963. I had just wandered into the store one Saturday afternoon to get out of the rain. I recall the store had a parrot in a cage right at the front that said hello to everyone who entered. I remember looking at a few fish and then some kittens.

But then I walked up to that little crate with a litter of Great Danes in it. They were all pretty small, and Barkley was the tiniest one. But man, when he looked up at me and I saw those big eyes, that was it. I knew I'd found something and someone special.

Barkley was the runt of a litter and I remember the pet store owners thought he would never get that big. They were wrong. Boy, were they wrong.

I took the tiny guy home and made a little bed for him on the floor right next to my bed. When it was time to go to sleep, he would just yelp all night. That's why I named him Barkley, by the way. He barked all the time.

Eventually, I picked him up and let him sleep in the bed. He would nuzzle right up next to me. It was adorable while he was tiny. But in no time at all, Barkley grew so big that his legs and paws hung off the sides of the bed. That guy was a real bed hog.

By the time he was six months old, he was bigger than any other dog I'd ever seen. At one year, he was the size of a small horse. People everywhere would remark about his size. I, of course, was quite used to it. Sure he was big, but he would always be my little puppy, my baby. Corny, I know.

We would walk beside the Arkansas River for miles most every night. The moon would reflect on that water, if there was any in the river. We'd walk through the park, into the woods and sometimes down to the river's edge. And if the water was way down, we'd go ahead and walk out onto the sandbars that formed in the middle of the river. Sometimes we would have to wade through water up to our knees, but nothing, and I mean nothing, made Barkley happier than getting out there on a sandbar. I'd let him off his leash and he'd take off like a racehorse across that shimmering sand kicking up clouds of dust behind him. He would hurdle branches and tires and all kinds of debris brought downstream by the river.

Out there in the pale moonlight, it was like we were in the middle of a small desert. Barkley would leave paw prints in his wake as he tore around the sandbar. I learned one day talking to an old timer who was fishing on the riverbank that some of the sandbars even had names. They were given titles like Miller's Sandbar, Ginny's Landing, Little Sahara. So I decided to name this particular one that he liked the most Barkley's Sandbar. It was our private joke.

Eventually, when Barkley would get tired of running around the sandbar and come running back to me, it was like a freight train trying to come to a stop. He'd basically run me over and then jump all over me and lick my face with that incredibly long tongue. I got soaked.

Now, just to be clear, we have all learned over the years that going out onto the sandbars is not all that safe. The water can rise suddenly and people have been trapped and even hurt out there. So please, be safe and don't go out on the sandbars.

Well, back to the story.

CHAPTER THREE

It was Christmastime 1964. Barkley and I were both single guys. I worked late too often, so when I got home, the big fella was ready for our walk. He would let me fix a TV dinner or make a sandwich, but was ready to go as soon as I finished, usually standing by the door with his leash hanging from his mouth.

That Christmas Eve, I had an office party that lasted until almost 10 o'clock. When I got home, Barkley was at the door waiting impatiently. He'd been alone all day and was ready to run and play. He didn't much care about the present I had bought and wrapped for him and put under the tree. He just wanted to run. I couldn't blame him.

So I changed into my walking shoes and a jacket. The temperature was in the 40s outside that evening, so not too cold at all. Barkley tugged at the leash as we walked out the front door and down the steps. I lived about three blocks from the Arkansas River, so it only took a few minutes to make it to the park along the river's edge.

I could see into many of the houses we passed. Christmas trees were lit up everywhere. Houses were decorated with lights and garland and bows. Most of the children were already in bed dreaming about what they'd find under their tree the next morning.

The weathermen had confirmed the bad news for the kids a couple of days earlier – it would not be a white Christmas this year. That was always a bummer, but just how it goes in Oklahoma. Sometimes we go an entire winter without snow. Other years we get several massive snowstorms with more than a foot of the white stuff. You never can tell.

Barkley and I had been walking for more than an hour and I was pooped, but he wanted to keep going. And since he had been cooped up all day, he deserved an extra long walk that night. It was just before midnight and I didn't much feel like hiking out onto his sandbar, but one look in his eyes told me he wouldn't be denied. So we trekked down the steep riverbank to the edge of the water and then I scrambled across a large log in the water to keep my feet dry on a cold night. Barkley just bounced and splashed through the water. He didn't care if it was chilly.

Once we made it over to the sandbar, I unsnapped Barkley's leash from his collar and watched him rocket across his personal little desert.

The usual process at this point would be for me to chase after him, maybe grab a stick and throw it for him to retrieve and then we would wrestle. He always won and I always ended up with sand down my neck and in my shoes and a soaking wet face from all his licking.

But this night was anything but usual. First of all, it was Christmas Eve. And second, what happened next was anything but normal or even believable.

I was out in the middle of the sandbar and Barkley was running around me like he was on a racetrack. Then he suddenly stopped. He basically skidded to a halt and cocked his head as he looked at me and then turned his massive head to look up at the night sky. About that time, I heard something as well and looked to the black night above. I couldn't see anything but stars.

I could just barely hear the faintest noise. It sounded like a chain rattling in the distance. And I thought I could also hear bells ringing. And then a moment later, I swore I heard someone yelling, shouting.

And then I saw something up there. Barkley saw it too and barked a few times. His loud, deep bark carried across the sandbar and the water. No way of telling what it was from that distance with only the dim light of the moon above. But it was definitely something. And it was coming our way.

"What the heck?" I said and Barkley whimpered in agreement.

I took a couple of steps toward Barkley and he started to back up toward me. He barked again. It was more like a howl this time. The rattling chains noise got louder and the shouting became clearer. I could hear a voice yelling out commands. It was a deep and booming voice. And for some reason, it was familiar, like I'd heard it before.

Several seconds later, I could see that whatever it was up there, it was coming down right at me and Barkley. I stepped over to him and patted his shoulder to keep him calm. But I was also ready to push him one way or the other if this thing continued its path directly at us.

And then it came into view. The dim moon provided just enough light to see it a little clearer. It was just a couple hundred feet away from us and coming in too fast. It was going to crash. The booming voice called out, "Whoa boys! Whoa now!" I didn't believe my eyes at first, who would? It was impossible.

I saw deer with horns and hooves and all. It was a group of deer and behind them was a sled and in the sled was a man. They were trying like heck to slow down as they plunged toward the sandbar. As they got closer, I could see they were all straining and the man in the sled was pulling hard on the reins.

The next part all happened in an instant. But you know how it is during very stressful events -- everything slowed down, like slow motion.

The deer and sled hit the ground with a tremendous noise, almost like an explosion, because they were traveling so fast. An enormous cloud of sand and dust shot up everywhere. I moved to the right and shoved Barkley a few feet as the team of deer and speeding sled shot out of the dust cloud and plowed right past us. They were all trying like heck to slow down. The deer were all pulling up and jamming their hooves into the sand. The gentlemen holding the reins was pulling back with all his might and yelling out, "That's it boys. Slow it on down now. Whoa!"

The whole thing -- the deer, the rattling chains and bells, the chubby man in red and the sled, all went right by Barkley and me in a blur, just a few feet in front of us. Then the whole mess finally came to a stop about 100 feet past us and not far from the water. I just stood there for a moment. I was frozen, dumbfounded, couldn't wrap my brain around what had just happened. Barkley pulled me out of my state of confusion when he took off toward the sleigh kicking up sand behind him.

I shook my head to try to wake up from this dream and then I found myself running after Barkley. When I got over to the sled, the chubby guy dressed in red had just jumped down onto the sand. He was petting Barkley between the ears where he liked it the most and calling him by his name.

CHAPTER FOUR

"That's a good boy, Barkley. Awfully good to see you," he was saying as he rubbed Barkley's head. Then he turned to me. "Great dog you have here Jerry." No one had called me Jerry since junior high when my dad passed away. I had been Gerald ever since then. And even in the dark of night with just the half moon over head I could see him wink at me.

"Thanks..." It was all I could stutter out. I was basically mesmerized. I took a step closer and then I stuttered some more, "Are you San...?... Can't be." I couldn't believe what I was seeing or what I was saying.

"Of course I am. Who else would be crazy enough to fly around in that contraption every year." And he turned away to walk up toward his stamping reindeer. "Darned lucky we didn't crash land a lot harder than we did. I knew the old fella was not right, but I had no idea he was this sick."

I followed him close behind. My head was still spinning, but this was really happening. Barkley was right next to Santa, sniffing at the reindeer as he walked by them. "What happened? Why did you crash?" I called to him. None of this could be real, but I still asked the question.

"Oh, it's Donner." Santa had reached the reindeer at the front of the line on the left. The poor guy was barely standing with his head full of horns just hanging there. Now, I'd never seen a sick reindeer, or any reindeer for that matter, but if there could be such a thing as a sick reindeer, poor Donner was one. And I'll be darned if that deer didn't sneeze.

"He picked up a cold last year at a stop in Siberia," Santa said while shaking his head. "Buford, my lead reindeer herder elf, and I thought Donner was in good enough shape to make the trip this year. But just look at him. He is barely standing on his four hooves." And then Santa bent down and laid his head on the reindeer's shoulder. You could tell without a doubt that he loved that animal.

When he turned back to me, jolly old Saint Nick was anything but. A tear was in his eye. "He's been with me the longest of them all in the team." He then stepped up to the lone deer at the front and patted him on the shoulder. "Young man, your father's going to be just fine. We'll just need to call it a night for this year and unload all the presents here so we can make it back home to the Pole." You could just hear the sadness in Santa's voice. He was heartbroken about having to leave his job unfinished. The reindeer all shook their heads and stamped. None of them wanted to go home either.

I have to admit it, the sight of Santa Claus standing there so forlorn brought tears to my own eyes. This should have been one of the happiest moments of my life. I mean come on, I was standing there talking to Santa Claus himself. This was fantasy kid stuff — the kind of thing every child dreams about.

But instead of joy and excitement and wonder, I too was deeply saddened that the rest of the children of the world would have to go without Christmas presents from Santa this year.

I couldn't help but think of me and my older brother Pete waking up on all those Christmas mornings. We'd wait anxiously at the top of the stairs in our pajamas giggling with anticipation until Dad and Mom called to us to come down. Then we'd fly down the stairs and burst into the living room and tear into the presents to see what Santa had brought us.

I don't know why, but for just a moment I thought about Mom. She had passed away three years earlier. It was almost 12 years to the day after Dad had died. She had never really gotten over losing him. I instinctively looked down at Barkley. I knew when I picked him up in that pet store two years ago that I was bringing him into my life to fill a hole left by losing my mother.

But back to Santa and the sandbar… I asked him, "Can't you just move Donner's son from the front to his father's spot and take off. Maybe you can just take a few presents off the sled and lighten the load a little."

Santa patted the young reindeer at the front again and then stepped back to me as I pet old Donner's shoulder. I was rustling my hand through his thick rough fur. "Jerry, I would definitely do that if I could. But it just doesn't work that way. You see, this sled, like the reindeers, is full of magic. Christmas magic. I don't even understand completely how it all works. It has just always been this way." And Santa proceeded to unhook Donner from his reins as he continued to talk to me.

"Things changed about a hundred years ago. You probably know the story and heard the song about that young fellow up front coming along."

"A hundred years ago?" I couldn't believe my ears.

And he laughed at me. It was a deep, rolling laugh with "ho, ho, ho" at the end. "Sure, you do realize I have been doing this job for more than a thousand years."

I stood there dumbfounded yet again. The look on my face caused Santa to laugh. "I've been making this trip since well before there was a billion people on the planet. Imagine how much tougher our job has gotten over the years as the population shot passed two, three, four and now more than five billion people. That means the elves, Mrs. Claus, the reindeer and I have to work incredibly hard year round preparing for this one night.

"Well, as I said, a hundred years ago, Donner's little guy was born. It was the first time we had ever had more than eight flying reindeer at one time. It had always been just eight for as long as I can remember. The average lifespan of one of these fellas is 300 years. This current team, that you likely know all their names, is third generation. Their parents and grandparents pulled the sled before they were born.

"Most of these guys have been with me on this trip hundreds of times. I figured that young 'un came along to allow us to travel faster and deliver more presents. It was the magic's way of fixing things."

"Three hundred years. I had no idea." I stood there with that same dumb look on my face just staring at Santa. I think Barkley had a similar look on his face but I couldn't be sure.

"Of course you didn't. Keeping everything a secret is part of the magic. Very few people in all the world in all of history know the true story."

I was suddenly struck by what he'd just said. I couldn't believe that of all the people in the world, I was one of a very select group that now knew Santa's secret. Why me?

"I'll bet you're thinking 'why me' aren't you Jerry?"

And just like that, Santa read my mind.

"Yes." Was all I could spit out.

"Well, I can tell you that no one who has ever learned the truth about me and the reindeer has ever told another person without my permission. For some reason, that is also part of the magic of all this. I never asked any questions when Christmas magic chose me to do this work and bring joy to children all around the world. I just understood that this is what the elves and I and these wonderful reindeer are supposed to do. We love it. I couldn't imagine anything better than doing what we do." And you could see that he was telling the truth. Santa truly loved what he did. He loved spreading joy and happiness to children all around the world. And I could also tell that he was deeply saddened to have to head home now with the job only half done.

He answered my next question without me even asking it. "I know what you're thinking, how can I just go home with the job not finished? Well Jerry, there are some things beyond even my control. And one of them is the fact that this sleigh weighs more than a million tons."

My mouth dropped wide open and my eyebrows got all squinched up. "A million tons? Two hundred million pounds? That's impossible." And I raised my hand to point at the sled. It was only maybe 10 feet wide and fifteen feet long. It couldn't hold more than a ton or two. It just couldn't.

Santa had Donner unhooked and began to walk him past me toward the sled. "No kidding Jerry. This little beauty here weighs more than a million tons right now. Well, at least it did when we left the North Pole to start our journey."

"No way. That's impossible."

"Oh, I know. Believe me. There is no way this sled could hold that many toys or possibly be moved even an inch with all that stuff loaded into it. But once again, it's the magic, Jerry. To be exact, it's that sack. It has the most magic of anything. Go take a look for yourself if you don't believe me." I just looked at him. "Go ahead, take a look." He added and gestured toward the sled.

So I stumbled over to the big red sleigh and climbed up into it. I rubbed my hand across its ancient polished wood. And I kneeled on the bench seat to reach the large sack behind it. I couldn't believe any of this, but there I was up in Santa's sled. So I reached up to the big brown sack made of some kind of shimmering fabric. I pried open the top to look down into it. What I saw surprised me more than anything I had seen up to this point. Down there inside the bag were millions, and I mean, millions of toys. It was like I could see a mile down into enormous stacks

21

and piles of toys and goodies. It looked like it went on forever. "Wow." It was all I could say.

CHAPTER FIVE

"I know. Wow." He chuckled. "That sack was the first thing Christmas magic brought to me. One morning a thousand years ago, I opened my door and there stood the elves with the sack. I knew right away what I was supposed to do."

Santa rubbed that famous white beard with his gloved hand and continued. "We first loaded that sack with toys that we made in the workshop. I knew we had made too many to take in one trip and I planned to come back to pick up the rest. But when we started loading things into the sack it just never got full. Ever. Over the years, we've loaded billions and billions of toys and books and bikes and dolls and everything you can ever imagine and the bag has never been full. Now that is the real magic."

I turned back to Santa. He was standing right there beside the sleigh. There was no smile on his face. He was very sad. He lived for nothing more than spreading joy.

Suddenly, I had an idea. "Santa, can't you just leave the presents for the kids in Tulsa here and I can deliver them for you. That should take away enough weight for the rest of the reindeer to finish the job." I was very excited about this plan. I thought it sounded like a great solution. I knew I could do it if I worked all night.

"Jerry, I really appreciate you volunteering like that. I always knew you'd turn out to be a great man." And then Santa did a most amazing thing. He took off his glove and put his bare hand on the side of my face and I swear a light started shining out of my skin where he touched me. "I wanted to tell you how sad I was to learn your father passed away back when you were 13. I know how hard that was for you and your brother. And then your mother a few years back." He smiled a pleasant smile that warmed my heart. "Believe me my boy. Your parents loved you very much and they are very proud of you today."

And then he answered my question again without me asking it. "Yes, that's part of the magic also. I get to hear and see every child in the world who ever lived over the past thousand years. Most children grow to become adults and grandparents but they are always children to me. I can see your parents right now when I look in your eyes. They loved you and your brother more than anything. You were the joy of their lives."

And that was it. My eyes, that had teared up a few minutes earlier, now started bawling. We're talking a waterfall of tears. I cried right there in front of Santa. He pulled me close and I put my head on his shoulder. Donner, standing beside him, nuzzled his snout against my leg. And Barkley rubbed his head against my other leg and whimpered.

Just then, enveloped by all that love, another idea came to mind. Tell you the truth, I think it was the Christmas magic that put the crazy idea in my jumbled up brain.

I raised my head off Santa's shoulder and looked from him to Donner and then to Barkley. I was no genius, but I could see that my huge nearly two-year-old Great Dane was as tall as that reindeer. I stepped back to get a better look and darned if I wasn't right. In fact, Barkley was maybe a couple of inches taller at the shoulder than that wonderful old reindeer.

Now, my idea about delivering the presents for Santa was a little crazy, but this one was a real doozy. "Santa, I have another idea."

I guess it was really insane because for the first time, Santa didn't know what I was thinking. He looked at me with that sad face. He was more than a thousand years old and had seen more than anyone in the world would ever see. But even he couldn't tell what I was thinking in that moment. "What's your idea Jerry?"

"I know this is crazy. But all of this is crazy, so what the heck."

He chuckled a little at my comment. "Go ahead."

"Well, you definitely have a problem here with one of your reindeer getting sick and not able to continue. What do you think about adding another reindeer?"

"Well, I'd love to. But I just don't see any extra reindeers around out here on this sandbar."

"How about a Great Dane reindeer?" I asked.

Santa's forehead got all wrinkled and his eyebrows squinched up. He looked from me to Barkley to Donner and then back to me. He brought a gloved hand up to his hairy white chin and rubbed it again. He looked at Barkley and then Donner a second time and then he shook his head and began to laugh. It was that booming "ho, ho, ho."

"Well I'll be." He stepped over to Barkley and patted him on the head and rubbed his ears. "He sure is a big fella, that's for sure."

"Biggest Great Dane most people have ever seen." I added.

"Looks like a strong one too."

"He pulls me around like a ragdoll on our walks. He could drag me from here to Texas if he wanted to."

Santa nodded his head. "Jerry. I have to admit, I would never have thought of this. But I just happen to know about a little secret stash of magic that I only get to use on the most special occasions. I can only use it in an emergency."

I smiled the biggest smile that had ever been on my face. "I think this is the definition of an emergency. This is Christmas for millions, heck, billions of kids we're talking about here, right?"

Santa looked up from petting Barkley and winked at me. "Yes indeed my boy. This is an emergency." So Santa stood up and hopped into his sled. He was amazingly quick and light on his feet. He grabbed a small bag and jumped back down. It was basically a miniature version of the infinite toy sack made of the same shimmering fabric. He took a couple of steps over to me. "Are you sure about this Jerry?"

"Absolutely." I immediately answered. He put his hand on my shoulder and nodded and then turned back to Barkley.

"Well boy. Here's your chance to save Christmas. Are you up to it?" And Barkley smiled his wonderful smile and jumped up in the air. He was raring to help. "Okay then. Let's see if there's still some magic in this bag." Santa reached his fingers into the small pouch and pulled out some glowing gold dust. He turned and winked at me again and then sprinkled the dust over Barkley. It fell slowly and seemed to sparkle as it landed on his fur.

CHAPTER SIX

For the briefest moment, Barkley changed from a white and black coat to a sparkly gold. And then a moment later he looked normal. He just stood there looking at Santa and then at me. It seemed that the magic didn't work. My excitement faded. My idea might not have been so great.

But Santa bent down to get his face at Barkley's level. I couldn't hear the words he whispered into Barkley's ear and I don't think I would have understood them even if I could hear. It sounded like he was speaking dog language. Then Santa stood up and stepped back a few steps. "Okay boy, go get em." And he threw his arm up.

Barkley took off running like he always does out here on the sandbar. But instead of tearing across the sand like normal, after a few steps, he was off the ground and rocketing up into the night sky. In a matter of seconds, he was up way past a hundred feet running, gliding through the air. He looked like a giant bird, like a rocket taking off, like a shooting star going the wrong way.

What he really looked like was a reindeer and he howled with pure delight as he flew through the air. It was without a doubt the single most incredible thing I had ever seen in my life. I burst out laughing and crying at the same time. Santa walked up and slapped my shoulder.

"My boy, this might just work." And then Santa took a couple of steps forward and whistled. "Come on boy, we've got some presents to deliver."

Barkley howled again as he came around and headed in for his landing. The sand shot up like a dust cloud as his paws hit the sandbar with a loud thud. Then he came running up to us and literally ran me over. I was on my back with him licking me all over the face. "Good boy. Good boy." Was all I could get out as he smothered me with dog kisses.

"Okay, up in the sled Donner." Santa had walked back to his eldest reindeer and helped him up into the sleigh. He came back up to us and walked Barkley over to Donner's spot in the reindeer brigade. Barkley obeyed his every command much better than he did any of mine, but it was Santa after all.

A few moments later, Barkley was harnessed at the front of the line with only Donner's son in front of him. My giant Great Dane turned to me with a look of pride that told me he was about to burst. His chest was puffed up bigger than I'd ever seen it. I stepped over and hugged him and patted him on the shoulder. "You'll do great boy. I'm proud of you fella. You do what Santa says, you hear?" He nuzzled up against my neck and then turned back to face forward. He had a job to do.

Santa had hopped back into the sled and grabbed the reins. "Jerry, I can't tell you how proud of you I am. A few hundred million children are darn lucky you and Barkley were out here on this sandbar tonight. I'm sure the Christmas magic had something to do with that. But I'm glad you were here. Now we've got to get going. Don't worry a bit about Barkley, I can tell he will hold his own with the reindeer."

I stepped back as they prepared to take off. "Good luck Santa." I couldn't think of anything more eloquent to say. So I just waved at him and Barkley. The other reindeer all turned and nodded at me as they prepared to pull the sleigh around the world.

I nodded to Santa and he shook the reins. He looked back at me and winked as he called out, "Okay boys, let's get back to business." He bellowed out a great rolling laugh of "ho, ho, ho." And then, as the sleigh started to pull forward he called out, "Come on boys, let's do your thing. On Dasher, on Dancer on Prancer, on Vixen. On

Comet, on Cupid, on Barkley and Blitzen." And as the reindeer team and the sleigh began to leave the sandbar behind, I heard Barkley howling with delight.

"You go boy." I whispered as the sleigh lifted into the night sky.

And then, just like that, it was quiet. I was all alone out there on Barkley's Sandbar with only the moon and stars overhead and the gentle trickling of the Arkansas River flowing by. I turned and walked back over to where I had taken Barkley's leash off of him. Before heading back home, I looked up again into the sky, but they were gone. My giant, lovable best friend was up there pulling Santa's sled and helping him complete his job this Christmas.

I hoped their crash landing out here on the sandbar didn't mess up their deliveries too much. I hoped they'd get all the toys delivered to the children around the world. It had taken about an hour to get them back up in the sky. I looked at my watch and was shocked yet again on this fantastically wonderful Christmas Eve.

The hands on my watch showed just minutes after midnight. The same time Barkley and I had come out here. I knew right away, the Christmas magic had frozen time. It was like it had all happened in a single tick of my watch.

Santa and the reindeer and my best friend Barkley were indeed going to make it. They were going to deliver all those presents to good little boys and girls around the world.

CHAPTER SEVEN

And there you have it. That's the story
of how my dog Barkley saved Christmas
in 1964. I know you have lots of
questions, and just like Santa could
read my mind that night nearly 50 years
ago, I'll answer some of your questions
now.

Yes, Barkley came back home. Two
days after Christmas that year, Barkley
woke me up by jumping up on my bed
and licking my face like he does every
morning.

I don't know where he came from or how he got in the house. He wasn't there when I went to bed the night before. But there he was that morning. I hugged and wrestled with him on the bed and then gave him his Christmas present he didn't get two days earlier. It was a big bone I had wrapped and put under the tree.

You probably want to know what happened to Barkley. Well, you most likely think he lived a good life and was with me for maybe 10 or 12 years, which is about the average lifespan for Great Danes. If you thought that, then you'll definitely be surprised to learn he is still with me. Yes, that's right. Barkley is still going strong almost 50 years later.

I guess the Christmas magic Santa sprinkled on him that Christmas Eve slowed down his aging, just like the reindeer. As far as I know, he is the world's oldest dog. But of course, I have kept that secret. Yes, my wife and kids and their kids have kept Barkley's secret too. We have had to fib a little to people and tell them Barkley is the son, grandson and now great grandson of the original.

And me? Yes I did meet my future wife less than a year after that amazing Christmas in 1964. We were married the following year and welcomed our first son in 1966. We had four children in all. They have all grown up and moved on and gotten married themselves . We welcomed our first grandchild in 1988. And we celebrated our first great grandchild earlier this year. I have truly had an amazing and wonderful life.

But life goes on and change is really the only thing that we can count on. My wife passed away just a couple of months ago and I have been pretty sick now for some time. But that happens when you get old. I have absolutely no regrets about my life. I have been blessed with love, friendship, family, children and a best friend I can always count on. And I have been very proud and blessed to be part of a miracle, a Christmas miracle.

I know what you're thinking now. You recall that Santa said the magic of Christmas has been kept a secret for more than a thousand years by the few who have learned about it. Well, I am one of those few lucky people. And now, so are you.

If you are reading this, then you must have found a bottle with a little story in it floating in the Arkansas River or the Mighty Mississippi or even in the ocean sometime after Christmas 2011.

You see, Santa told me it was okay to share my story with one other person because the magic of Christmas needs to be passed on to others who will cherish and protect and carry on the spirit of the season. Keeping the secret is part of Christmas magic. And that magic chose you.

If you found the bottle, then I am gone. Just after midnight, Santa and his reindeer, with a replacement for old Donner, landed on Barkley's Sandbar just like they did almost 50 years ago. Barkley and I were given one of the greatest gifts in all the world. I joined Santa on the sleigh and Santa hitched Barkley up at the very front of the reindeer brigade.

When he came back to sit beside me in the sleigh I finished writing you this story. I'm going to roll these pages up and stuff them in the bottle in just a moment.

Believe it or not, as I write this, Santa is handing me the reins and laughing his "ho, ho, ho" laugh. So I will say goodbye to you and wish you all the wonder and joy and happiness in the world. And even though I have never met you and probably never will, I am trusting you with the magic of Christmas.

Before I go, I have to tell you, I am just about to shout out those famous reindeer names when this sled takes off. Wow!

Good luck to you. Barkley and Santa and I wish you a Merry Christmas, a Happy New Year and a wonderful life.

ABOUT THE AUTHOR AND STORY

Chris Metcalf lives near the Arkansas River in Oklahoma. He and his wife Diana have five kids. The Holiday Season is always a big deal around the Metcalf household. Barkley's story was written on Christmas Eve in 2010. It was inspired by a neighbor who walked (really, they walked her) a couple of very large Great Danes around our neighborhood.

I know your first question. Why didn't the story mention a certain reindeer with a distinctive facial feature? That famous character (Donner's son) is still under copyright by its owners. That means leaving the character out of this story keeps the author from receiving letters from nice attorneys.

I hope you enjoyed this story. I think we may be in for a few more Barkley adventures in the coming years. Merry Christmas and Happy Holidays from Barkley and me.

SANDBAR SAFETY WARNING

As Gerald mentioned in the story, the sandbars that form in the Arkansas River are no place to play. The water level in the river can rise rapidly without warning and people have been trapped and needed to be rescued. People have been washed downstream and drowned. Please be safe and stay off the sandbars.

Made in the USA
Charleston, SC
08 December 2011